P9-DGL-974

Listen for the Bus
David's Story

by Patricia McMahon

with photographs by John Godt

Boyds Mills Press

Acknowledgments

I offer my most sincere gratitude to the Power family—Dave, Helene, and David (and welcome, Colin!). Without their courtesy and generosity, I would have no story to tell. They have my admiration along with my thanks.

I want to thank David's teachers, Barbara Magee and Jackie Boudreau, for welcoming me into their classroom, and everyone else at the Willard School. The administration, faculty, and students were all so open and helpful. Particular thanks go to all the students in Mrs. Magee and Ms. Boudreau's classroom, who so nicely ignored John and me.

I send my thanks to Maryann Morran of the Concord Public Schools, Concord, Massachusetts, who aided and abetted me (from one T.B. to another).

I must also thank the administration of the Concord Public Schools—Thomas Scott, superintendent—for its support.

Kind assistance was provided by Tracy Evans of the New England Center for Deaf-Blind Studies; Jero Nesson of the Emerson Umbrella for the Arts, Concord, Massachusetts; Donovan Godt, who sent her dad; and Conor Clarke McCarthy, who shared his first week of kindergarten.   — P.M.

Text copyright © 1995 by Patricia McMahon
Photographs copyright © 1995 by John Godt
All rights reserved

Published by Caroline House
Boyds Mills Press, Inc.
A Highlights Company
815 Church Street
Honesdale, Pennsylvania 18431
Printed in Mexico

Publisher Cataloging-in-Publication Data
McMahon, Patricia.
   Listen for the bus : David's story / by Patricia McMahon ;
with photographs by John Godt.—1st American ed.
[48]p. : col. ill. ; cm.
Summary : A real-life look at David, who is blind, as he begins kindergarten.
ISBN 1-56397-368-5
1. Children, blind—Juvenile literature. 2. Visually handicapped children—Juvenile literature.
3. Kindergarten—Juvenile literature. [1. Blindness. 2. Kindergarten.] I. Godt, John, ill. II. Title.
362.41—dc20   [E]   1995   CIP
Library of Congress Catalog Card Number 94-73316

First edition, 1995
Book designed by Karen Donovan Godt
The text of this book is set in 14-point Palatino.

10 9 8 7 6 5 4 3 2

Because of deep love, one is courageous.

— *Lao Tzu*

This book is for Helene Power,
a woman of courage. A small gift from
one mother to another.   — P.M.

To Donovan, who teaches me new ways
to see every day.   — J.G.

Summer is not quite over, fall is creeping up fast.
And the school year has begun again. Newly washed yellow buses make
their morning runs, delivering children to brightly decorated classrooms.
One wall of one kindergarten, the room where Mrs. Magee and
Ms. Boudreau teach, is covered with big colored paper circles. Each circle
contains a picture of one of the children in the class. Underneath the
picture is a list each child has made of his or her favorite things.

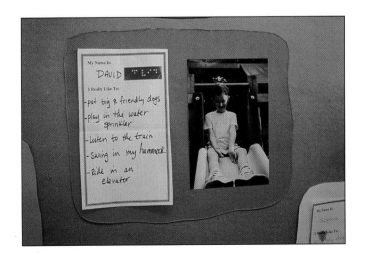

One list belongs to a boy whose name is written in two ways. His list says he likes big dogs, water sprinklers, the hammock swing, listening to the train, and riding in elevators. The picture in his circle shows a smiling boy who is just ready to fly down a slide. His name is David.

School is not listed as one of the things David likes best. But that's because David made the list at the end of summer. Right now, school is a place that makes David very happy. His classroom is full of children, full of exciting sounds, and full of curious shapes to hold, to feel, and to play with. Each day brings something new.

In the mornings, David's mother walks with him to the end of their driveway to wait for the bus. She waves as she sees it coming. David hears the big sound of the engine as it comes close, hears the brakes squeal as it stops. He doesn't see the bus because David is blind. His eyes do not work.

His legs, however, work just fine. His mother helps him find the handrail, get his balance, and climb onto the bus. David hears his mother saying good-bye. He likes to hear the children who know him call out "Hi, David!" He smiles as he feels the bus pulling away from home, going to school.

In the classroom,
all the children know it's "first things first."
David puts his knapsack, which feels
so bulky on his back, in his cubby.
David finds his cubby with his hands.
The teachers have lined it with corrugated
cardboard. This is knobby stuff that is
easy to feel with his hands.
It makes a noise when he runs his
fingers fast along it.

Children in the class like to meet David at his cubby.

They like to see if they can help.

Ms. Boudreau helps David find
the "I am here" board. David's star has
bumpy edges. He feels the bumps and knows
this is his star, not someone else's.

David's star has his name written two ways,
just like his picture. The dots spell David's name
in a kind of writing known as Braille.
Braille was invented so that people who could not
use their eyes to read could use their hands instead.
The dots in patterns make letters; the readers
feel them with their fingers. David will learn which
groups of dots make which letters. Then he
will learn which letters go together to make words.
Just the way the other children in his class learn letters
and then make them into words.

One day in circle time, there is important
work to do. The class is building a terrarium.
The teachers, Mrs. Magee and Ms. Boudreau,
asked the children to bring plants, rocks,
dirt, and grass—all to make a small
growing world in a glass box. The teachers
have brought snails that will make
the terrarium their home.

David has brought a rock that he
and his mother found yesterday afternoon.
His mother helped him place it in a small
plastic container to bring to school.

Before school, David and his mother, Helene, talked about the rock.
They used a different language called sign language. David can hear, but
not as well as most children. His hearing aid helps a lot. Because he does
not hear well, David's learning to speak has gone slowly. But like all
children, David needs words to say what he thinks or wants or knows.
So he talks using sign language.

At school, Ms. Boudreau helps David find the terrarium.
David uses his hands to find the shape—the edge, the inside,
and the outside. He places his rock inside, signing "rock."
The other children practice signing, learning from David
a different way to make words.

A kindergarten day for David is busy and full.
There is circle time, story time—which is one of David's
favorites—and then snack, which is always a good time.
Friends sit down to eat treats from home.
Then there is playtime, when David joins the plastic-block
builders. David turns the blocks over and over in his hands.
He learns that the blocks are hard, that they have sharp edges
and bumpy tops, and that he can put his fingers inside
from the bottom. With time and careful feeling, David learns
that one block can fit on top of another and stay there.

A little later, Ms. Boudreau watches and waits
to help David work with soft clay. David explores
the roller, which is hard, round, smooth, and a little bit long.
Banging it on the table makes a loud sound, a sound that
makes Ms. Boudreau say, "Softer, please, David."
Soft clay is sticky, soft like its name, with a sweet sort of smell.
The clay moves when David pushes his hands into it.

But the roller does not. David thinks about this.
He is excited about working with the soft clay and the hard roller.
He moves his body from side to side. Along with his smile,
this is one of the ways David shows he is happy.

The soft-clay table is now one of
David's special places in the classroom.
He has a new favorite thing to add to his list.

When David comes home from school,
his mother is always there to meet him.
Every afternoon his teachers send home a
book telling about David's day at school.
Today, David and Helene sit together in the
beginning-of-the-school-year warm afternoon sun.
They are talking about school. David and his
mom remember the terrarium and the clay table,
which brings out a David smile. Helene shows
David once more how to sign "book."

David's mother, like so many mothers, hugs
her boy each time he comes home from school.
David, like so many other children, is happy to be home.

And when he's home,
David loves to go outside in his backyard.
At lunch, David signs the word "swing"
to his mother. Together they go outside
to David's swing set. David is never
anything but happy when he's swinging.
Higher and higher he likes to go.
When his mother's arms get tired
and the swing slows down, David signs,
"More! More!" Helene checks to see
what David is signing; she helps him
put his hands just right. But David
doesn't want to practice signing.
He wants to go fast. He wants to feel the
air as it rushes past his face. As Helene
pushes him again and again,
she thinks that swinging high and fast
should have been number one on
David's list of favorite things.

After playing, they go inside for a snack. David's mother tells him that she is opening the refrigerator and getting his juice. She reminds him that the juice is inside the refrigerator, cold and waiting. David finds his chair. He sits down and enjoys the juice, some raisins, and his mother's happy voice.

Just before dinner, David likes to walk with his father. They almost always head across the street to their neighbors' house, where the big dog lives. Mikey comes running and jumping when he sees David.

David begins to laugh
and rock when he hears him.
He uses his hand against his leg
to sign the word "dog."
David loves the softness of
the dog's fur, his wet, sloppy kisses,
the cold of his nose, and the loud
noise of his happy bark.
David pushes, pats, rubs, and tries
to hug him; his dog friend
never seems to mind.
Mikey is sometimes so glad to see
David that he knocks him over
with a big-dog welcome.
David never seems to mind.

On the way home David signs,
"Swing." David's father knows that his
son doesn't mean the backyard swing.
Dave, the father, and David have a
swing of their own. Dave picks up David,

turning him into a human swing.
Back and forth, back and forth,
wilder and wilder, until the swinger,
or the swing, gives up.

Dave and David are laughing as they play their favorite father-and-son game.

One afternoon a week, David and Helene
scurry a bit after school. They are heading to a farm
near town, and they want to be on time.
David has been going to this farm to ride horses since
he was two years old. David's list of favorite things
should have said "big dogs and bigger horses."

With a helmet on for safety, David climbs up onto
the broad back of his favorite horse. The teacher reminds
David to hold on. She guides the horse by running
around the paddock as fast as she can. David, bouncing
along happily on the horse's broad back, wants more.
Forgetting to hold on, he lets go to sign, "Faster, faster."

When his riding time
is done and Helene lifts him down,
the joy of riding fills his face.

On the way home from the farm,
David and his mother stop to do the grocery
shopping. Although not nearly as much fun as riding,
pushing the shopping cart is still a good game.
David knows how to take the groceries down from
the shelf, find the edge of the cart, and lower
the groceries in. Inside, not out. David hears the sound
breakfast cereal makes as he drops it into
the cart, just like the sound the cereal makes when
it falls into the bowl at breakfast time.

Near the grocery store is the
train station. Children in David's
town love to go there. As David's list
says, he loves to hear the train come in.
As he waits, the sound gets bigger
and bigger, closer and closer, louder
and louder. As the train gets
oh-so-close, right in front of him,
David laughs and rocks at the great,
grand noisiness of it. The boy next
to him covers his ears; he's a little bit
nervous about a noise that large.
But David loves the sound and
the way he can feel the
ground shaking beneath him.

Rumbling sounds and loud banging
sounds are exciting to David—as long
as they are not too big a surprise.
A noise without warning startles
David, as it would anyone. But certain
noises, and the feeling that goes
with them, are just plain fun.

David's father knows this well.
One day he finds David in his room
listening to music. He tells David
the back door needs fixing,
fixing with a hammer and a nail.
David smiles. Hammers are among
David's favorite things. While David's
father bangs the hammer, David holds on
to his father. The hammering shakes
all the way through his father
and all the way through David.
This makes David laugh out loud.
Then David takes a turn.

He hears the noise made by the
heavy shape called a hammer.
The banging shakes right through
the hammer into David's hand.
Bang, *bang* again.
David and Dave banging.
Laughing and banging.

Four hands banging on a piano make another sound
David loves. He plays, in his own way, with his father or
his mother. Sometimes he just leans against his father
while his father plays the notes that make a tune.
One afternoon, David's father stops before David wants
him to. David bangs the piano. He signs, "More."

Then he signs, "More" again. But David's father doesn't
see David's words. He calls out that he'll be right back.

David doesn't realize his father hasn't seen his words.
David becomes angry and sad, an all-mixed-up feeling.
David calls out, loud and complaining.

His mother comes to see what is wrong,
trying to understand why David feels so sad.
She hugs him, the way mothers do.

That night David's mother makes
one of David's favorite dinners.
Helene reminds David to keep one hand
on his plate all the time. This way David
knows where his plate is. And his fork
is more likely to find his meat.
Helene always places David's milk in the
same spot so David can reach out and
easily find it. David's mother sits and talks
with him — about the day at school, about
where the spoon is for applesauce. They
practice signing the words for David's food.

At the end of dinner, David heads for his
hammock swing, the one from his list.
He curls up, thinking his David thoughts,
some happy, some maybe not so.
Later his parents find him there, all
worn out and sleeping.

In the morning, it's back to school again.
Ms. Boudreau meets David's bus, as one of his teachers
or classmates always does. She helps David retrace the path to
the classroom. David "trails" his hand along the walls.
He remembers that the brick wall leads to the corner.
There he turns, and another brick wall leads to the heavy door.

Inside the door, a thick mat feels fat underfoot.
Beyond the mat there is another door, a short wall, and then
the cubbies. David finds the one with the knobby paper.
A friend says, "Hi, David, I'm here." So David knows.

At circle time, Mrs. Magee goes over the schedule for the day.
Gym today. Yesterday was art. Tomorrow is music. David knows his art
class by the yarn on the door. Next to the yarn, the Braille letters spell "art."

Yarn means the day Ms. Boudreau
will help him trail down a long hall, the
one with the radiator. David likes to
hit the radiator, making a great noise.
He laughs all the way to art class.
A wood block in the morning means
gym today. This morning, while
waiting for the bus, Helene gave
David the wood block Ms. Boudreau
had sent home last night. David holds
and explores the mostly smooth,
a-little-bit-sticky hardwood block.

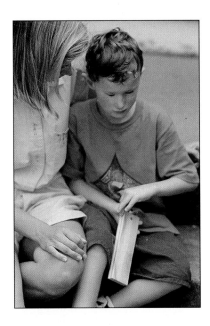

Later, in the gym, David feels the floor with his hands.
Mostly smooth, a little bit sticky, and hard. David learns.

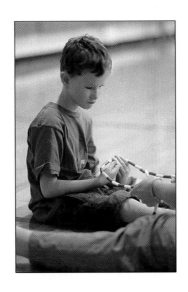

In gym class, the other children do some running while David practices
walking fast. The gym teacher passes out jump ropes. Some children jump rope
by themselves. Some make their ropes into letter shapes. One boy
makes a jump rope circle and sits safely inside. Three girls jump rope together.
David explores. He discovers something long, made up of smaller pieces—
something new called a jump rope.

After school, David waits on line for the bus with the other children.
The bus windows are open today. As the bus heads home, warm wind whistles
past the open windows. The seat crackles as David moves around on it. The bus
makes a clanking, complaining sound every time it slows down. Some children
are singing a song about Batman. David smiles.

If he were to make a new list
of his favorite things, "riding the bus"
would come right after "big dogs."

Home to his mother,
home to lunch. David remembers
his gym class, the gym floor.
He pauses to check the feel of grass
under one foot, the feel of stone under
the other. Right through his shoes,
David is learning to tell where
he's standing. Soon leaves will
begin to fall. David will feel
their lovely crackle underfoot.

   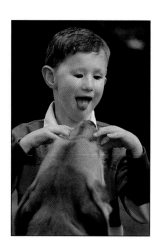

But for now, after school, it's time for lunch.
Then a book with his mother, words read out loud
and words to feel in Braille. Or a swing, or maybe a
music tape. Later, when David's father comes home,
there may be enough time for the evening walk.
The one that always leads to the dog.
Or perhaps the piano instead.

Or, too tired, maybe this boy will fall asleep,
swinging softly in his favorite hammock chair.
Tired, happy, and David. At the end of another day.